GB MAR 1 0 1992

R00089 99928

P9-AOH-904

E Stevenson

Stevenson, James, 1929-

Mr. Hacker /

c1990.

PALM BEACH COUNTY
LIBRARY SYSTEM
3650 SUMMIT BLVD
WEST PALM BEACH, FL 33406

© THE BAKER & TAYLOR CO.

MR. HACKER

by James Stevenson
pictures by Frank Modell

PALM BEACH COUNTY
LIBRARY SYSTEM
3650 SUMMIT BLVD
WEST PALM BEACH, FL 33406

GREENWILLOW BOOKS, New York

For Wolfie
—J.S.

For Suçie
—F.M.

Watercolor paints and a black pen
were used for the full-color art.
The text type is Brighton Medium.

Text copyright © 1990 by James Stevenson
Illustrations copyright © 1990 by Frank Modell
All rights reserved. No part of this book
may be reproduced or utilized in any form
or by any means, electronic or mechanical,
including photocopying, recording, or by
any information storage and retrieval
system, without permission in writing
from the Publisher, Greenwillow Books,
a division of William Morrow & Company, Inc.,
105 Madison Avenue, New York, NY 10016.

Printed in Singapore by Tien Wah Press

First Edition   10 9 8 7 6 5 4 3 2 1

Library of Congress Cataloging-in-Publication Data

Stevenson, James (date)
Mr. Hacker / by James Stevenson ;
pictures by Frank Modell.
            p.   cm.
Summary: Mr. Hacker begins to regret his move
from the noisy city to the quiet country, until
he is befriended by a stray cat and dog.
ISNB 0-688-09216-0.
ISBN 0-688-09217-9 (lib. bdg.)
[1. Loneliness—Fiction.]
I. Modell, Frank, ill.   II. Title.
PZ7.S84748Mr   1990
[E]—dc20   89-30479   CIP   AC

CONTENTS

1. THE CITY

Old Mr. Hacker lived alone in the city.
He used to like it, but not anymore.
The people upstairs were always making a racket.
Somebody played a loud radio next door.
The elevator was often broken, and the stairs were
hard to climb.

The streets were full of garbage.
The places where Mr. Hacker used to shop were closed.
He hardly ever saw any faces he knew.
"I wonder what it would be like to live in the country?"
he said to himself.
At night he began to dream of villages and fields, and
of wind moving through the branches of big trees.

2. MOVING

In the middle of the summer, Mr. Hacker left the hot
city and moved to a small house in the country.
The moving men carried his furniture into the empty
rooms, said good-bye, and drove away.
Mr. Hacker stood on his front porch and looked
at the road.
Then he went into his backyard.
There were apple trees and a garden grown wild.
He looked across a field. In the distance were a
few houses.
It was very quiet.

3. LONELY

After a few weeks, Mr. Hacker was so lonely he wished
he were back in the city. He missed the noises and the
smells and all the people.

"Too late now," he said to himself.

He glared at the apple trees dropping their apples—
thud, thud—on the grass.

4. THE YELLOW CAT

One morning Mr. Hacker looked out the window of his
living room. A big yellow cat was crouching on the porch.
When the cat saw Mr. Hacker, it ran away.
The next morning the same cat was on the porch again.
Mr. Hacker crept into the kitchen and put some milk in
a dish. Then he crept back and slowly opened the door
to the porch.
The cat dashed off.
Mr. Hacker put the dish of milk on the porch.
In the afternoon the dish was empty.
Mr. Hacker filled the dish again.
By evening the milk was gone again.

5. THE LARGE BROWN DOG

The next day Mr. Hacker went to the store and
bought some cat food.
He put a bowl of cat food and a bowl of milk
on his porch.
Then he went inside and waited by the window.

A large, brown, dirty-looking dog walked up onto
the porch.
It looked around.
Then it ate the cat food, drank the milk, and strolled
away down the road.
"My goodness," said Mr. Hacker.

Then the yellow cat arrived.

The cat looked at the empty bowls and started
to leave.

"Wait," called Mr. Hacker, opening the door,

"I'll get some more."

The cat ran away.

6. DOG FOOD, CAT FOOD

The next morning Mr. Hacker made another trip to
the store.

He bought a bag of dog food and a box of dog bones.

At one side of the porch, he put a bowl of dog food
and a dog bone and a bowl of water.

At the other side of the porch, he put a bowl of cat
food and a bowl of milk.

When he looked out the window, he saw the yellow cat
creeping onto the porch. The cat sniffed at the dog food,
then walked over to the cat food and began to eat.
"Now I've done it right," said Mr. Hacker.
Just then the cat stopped eating, looked around, and
dashed off.

The dirty-looking dog appeared, ate the dog food, the dog bone, the cat food, drank the milk and some of the water, too.

Mr. Hacker went out onto the porch. "You shouldn't have done that," said Mr. Hacker.

The dog looked at him and wagged its tail.

Mr. Hacker collected all the bowls and went inside.

The dog scratched at the door.

"Go home," said Mr. Hacker. But he was pretty sure the dog didn't have a home. It didn't even have a collar.

"Go someplace," said Mr. Hacker.

After a while the dog wandered away.

Then the yellow cat came back. But there were
no bowls on the porch.
"Wait," called Mr. Hacker.
The cat ran off.

7. INTO THE HOUSE

For the next few days, Mr. Hacker was very busy trying to get the right food to the right animal at the right time. Sometimes it worked, but mostly it didn't.

The dirty-looking dog seemed to be getting fatter, and the yellow cat skinnier.

One evening as the dog arrived, Mr. Hacker had an idea. He picked up the dog bowl and the dog bone, and carried them into the house. The dog came right after him, wagging its tail.

Mr. Hacker put the food on the kitchen floor. The dog ate it up.

Mr. Hacker held the front door open. "Out you go," he said. The dog looked at the open door. Then it jumped up onto the sofa and lay down.

"You can't stay here," said Mr. Hacker. The dog closed its eyes. "You can't," said Mr. Hacker. The dog wagged its tail, and soon it was asleep.

Mr. Hacker sat watching the dog. When it woke up, Mr. Hacker went to the door and opened it. "Out you go," he said again.

The dog jumped off the sofa and went right out.

Mr. Hacker closed the door. "Perfect," he said, and he went to bed.

Just as he was turning out the light, he heard scratching at the door.

8. SNOW

Two months later, Mr. Hacker was putting cat food out on the front porch for Ellie, the yellow cat—who came by twice a day now and wasn't afraid of anything—when snow began to fall.

"Look at that, Jarvis," he said to the dog, who lived in the house now, and was much cleaner, and slept on the sofa at night. "Maybe I should put out some food for the birds."

Mr. Hacker and Jarvis looked out the back window,
watching the snow fly past the apple trees.
"A little bird seed couldn't hurt," said Mr. Hacker.

28

9. "HERE WE GO AGAIN"

The next day Mr. Hacker put up a bird feeder and filled
it with seed. Then he and Jarvis went indoors to see
if the birds would notice.

A gray squirrel ran down the apple tree and jumped onto the bird feeder. In a moment all the bird seed was gone. The squirrel ran up the tree.

A couple of birds flew over to the bird feeder, but they didn't stay long.

"Well," said Mr. Hacker, "here we go again!"

Mr. Hacker and Jarvis walked to the store.

Mr. Hacker bought some cat food, dog food, dog bones,

bird seed, and—for the squirrels—a bag of nuts.

Then he and Jarvis walked home through the snow.

32